He lived in a trailer
with his dad, Bolivar, king of the acrobats.

Bavarotti, the performing elephant,

was his best friend.

When Thomas grew up, he wanted to work at the circus.
Just like his dad. And his dad's dad.

But it was so hard to do circus tricks. So much work!
So much training! So many things to learn!

And to tell you the truth, Thomas was clumsy,

very clumsy.

"I'm good for nothing" was what Thomas thought at last.
"The circus will never have me."

And he left the circus
and Bavarotti the Elephant
and his dad,
and went off to look
for another job.

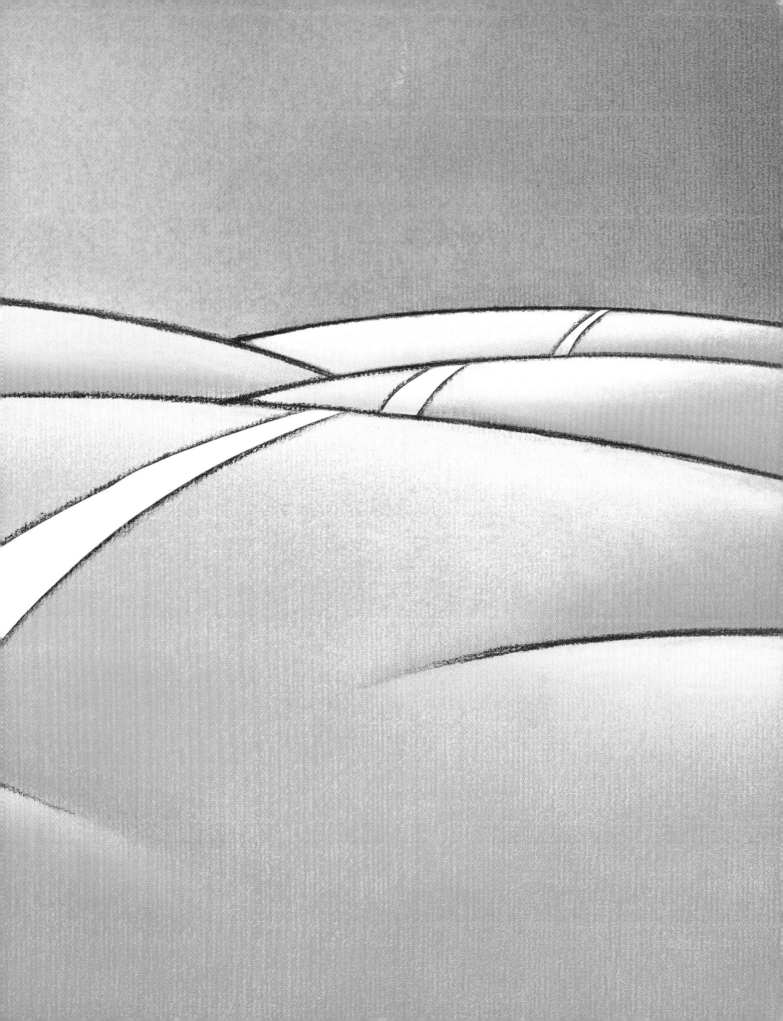

That night, Thomas was all alone.
He slept on his troubles.

Go back home,
a star whispered to Thomas.
Go home where they need you.

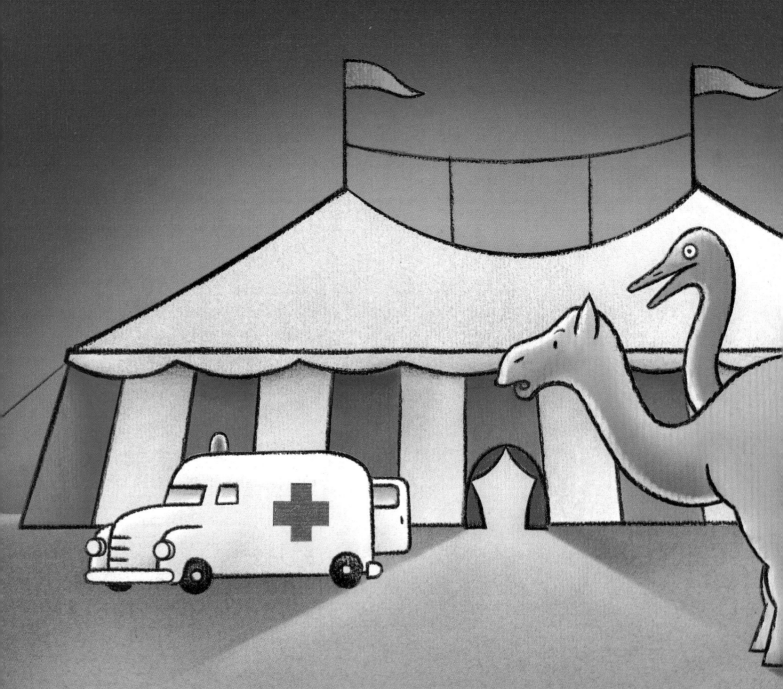

Thomas hurried back to the circus. That night's show had already begun. But something had happened. Something bad.

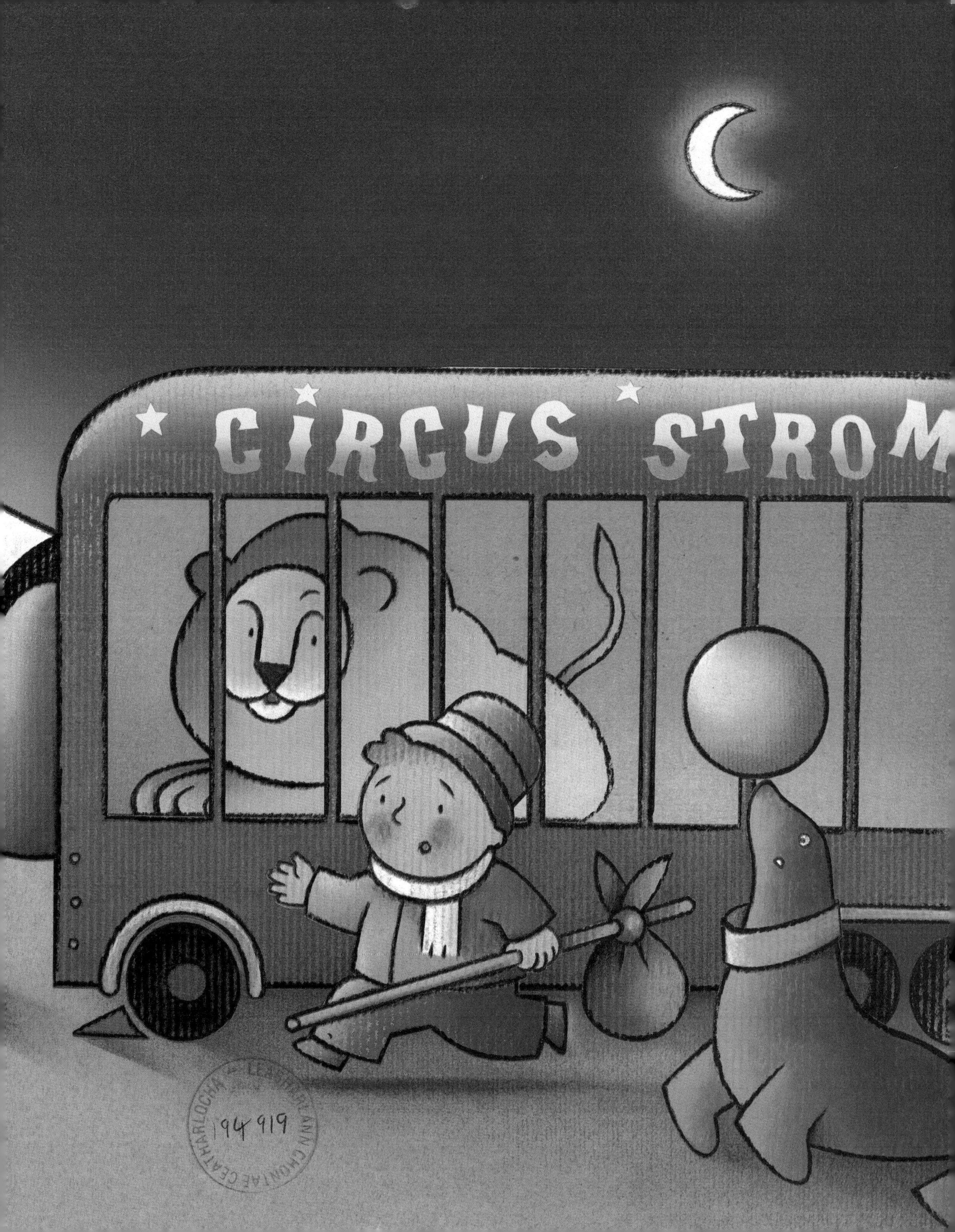
CIRCUS STROM

Thomas ran to the Big Top.
Bavarotti was in pain. In great pain.
And no one could help.

No one except Thomas.
He saw what it was right away.
Bavarotti was saved.
The show could go on!

What a great day for Thomas.
The *bravos!* The *hoorays!*
With his dad's arms around him
Thomas knew exactly what he'd be when he grew up.

"An animal doctor is the job for me," he said.
"I will take care of all my friends, elephants especially."
And when he grew up, that's just what he did.